TASK FORCE DELTA

ROGUE PREDATOR

Craig Simpson

Text © Craig Simpson 2012

Cover design by Peter Scoulding

Franklin Watts
338 Euston Road
London NW1 3BH

Franklin Watts Australia
Level 17/207 Kent Street
Sydney, NSW 2000

A CIP catalogue record for this book
is available from the British Library.

ISBN: 978 1 4451 0694 6

1 3 5 7 9 10 8 6 4 2

Printed in Great Britain

Franklin Watts is a division of Hachette Children's Books,
an Hachette UK company.
www.hachette.co.uk

The Real Delta Force

Task Force Delta is inspired by one
of the United States' top-level secret
military units, the 1st Special Forces
Operational Detachment — Delta (1SFOD-D)

also known as

Delta Force

Delta Force's main missions are direct, counter-terrorism
action. They also carry out many secret assignments
including hostage rescues and raids behind enemy lines.

Delta Force (also called "The Unit")
is based at Fort Bragg, Carolina, USA.

Delta Force's motto is:
"Surprise, Speed, Success"

Major Nathan Connor
Highly decorated
Commander of Delta Force.
Transferred from the 75th
Ranger Regiment. Speaks
five languages including
Pashto.

Lieutenant Danny Crow
Second in command.
Came top of his class in Special Forces'
"Operative Training Course".

Lieutenant Jacko Alvarez
A former Navy Seal and
weapons expert.

Sergeant Major Sparks
Comms and intel expert and
veteran of several Special
Forces units before being hand-
picked for Delta Force.

**Master Sergeant
Ben Saunders**
Transferred from 75th
Ranger Regiment. An
expert in survival skills
and demolition.

**Sergeant First Class
Sam Wilson**
World-class sniper skills led to
recruitment into Delta Force,
despite being just 19 (usual
minimum age 21).

CONTENTS

CHAPTER ONE
Code Red

Fort Brannigan US Air Force base, Nevada desert

A voice crackled through Flight Lieutenant Travis's earpiece.

"Predator Alpha One, this is Halo Forward Patrol. High Value Targets heading south towards Mazar-e-Sharif... Three red Toyota pickups kicking dust. Local intel confirms occupants are Taliban... Proceed with Operation Demon and engage, over."

Travis sat in his leather fighting chair. He watched the convoy on a row of TV screens in front of him. The live images were beamed thousands of miles from Afghanistan via satellite to the safety of his blast-proof Ops Room. "Roger that, Halo Forward Patrol. I have positive visual ID from Predator Alpha One, over."

Travis popped a fresh piece of gum into his mouth and began chewing. He was in charge of the coolest computer combat game ever; the coolest in the world because it was real. His Predator Unmanned Combat Aerial Vehicle, called a drone, was circling the sky in Afghanistan at ten thousand feet. Travis was going into battle.

He needed to focus. He shut out the annoying hum of computers in the Ops Room.

The Predator's controls resembled those in a fighter plane. He gripped the joystick and applied gentle pressure. The drone responded to his commands after precisely one and a half seconds. That's the time it took for the signal to bounce via satellite.

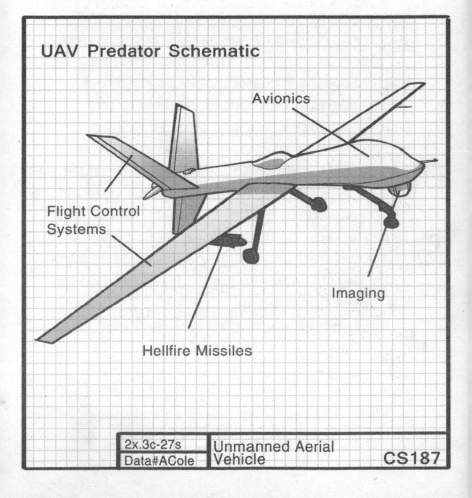

UAV Predator Schematic

Avionics

Flight Control Systems

Imaging

Hellfire Missiles

2x.3c-27s	Unmanned Aerial	
Data#ACole	Vehicle	CS187

Travis began the Predator's descent; reducing height and closing on the target vehicles. The latest digital cameras on the Predator became his electronic eyes. The cameras could read number plates, track vehicles, and even evaluate suspect locations for IEDs — improvised explosive devices — the roadside bombs dreaded by all soldiers on the ground. Best of all though, were the Predator's impressive weapons. The drone was armed with Hellfire air-to-ground missiles. Perfect.

"Steady as she goes," Travis muttered. He levelled out the Predator at five hundred feet. "Nice and easy." He reduced airspeed to one hundred miles per hour and armed a Hellfire missile. Then he zoomed in the camera on the Toyotas. He locked on to the middle of the three pickups by activating his laser-guidance system. "Halo Forward Patrol, this is Predator Alpha One. Target locked. About to engage. Just sit back with a cool beer and watch the show. You all have a nice day now. Over and out." Travis reached for the missile-firing button.

The screens blinked, pixelated, and went blank. Travis's jaw froze. "What the...?" He pressed a few buttons. Nothing. He swivelled round. "Hey, you guys, is there a glitch with the sat-link?" The tech guys looked up and shook their heads. "Then, what the—?" Suddenly the screens came alive again.

"One of these days those goddamn gremlins will give me a heart attack," Travis joked, hiding his relief. "*Adios amigos*." He leaned forward and pressed the missile firing button.

Nothing happened. He pushed the button again. Still nothing. The image on the screen drifted away from the convoy of pickups. Panic stricken, Travis had to think fast; either the camera had a mind of its own or the drone was altering course. Both possibilities pointed to a serious malfunction. He no longer had control.

"Code Red," Travis called out in alarm. "We've got a rogue Predator... Aborting mission." He lifted a flap which concealed the self-destruct switch. He flicked it. The screen should have gone blank as the Predator blew itself up. Instead, what unfolded before his eyes drained the blood from his face. The drone's targeting system had locked on to the men of Halo Forward Patrol. Travis let go of the joystick and clasped his head with both hands. "No!" he cried out as the drone's weapon system confirmed missile launch. Shaking, Travis fumbled for his phone and its direct line to three-star General Patterson, Head of Central Command.

CHAPTER TWO
An old friend

North of Mazar-e-Sharif, Afghanistan

Earlier that morning, Delta Force's commander, Major Nathan Connor, ordered his armoured Humvee to stop. Its heavy duty all-terrain tyres bit into the dirt and it skidded to a halt. They could see the remote village in front of them. Lieutenant Jacko Alvarez turned off the noisy engine. In the silence Connor scanned the area. Nothing had changed — the place was just how he remembered it. Volunteering for the mission had seemed such a good idea. Now, he was less sure.

Connor knew Halo Forward Patrol were positioned on a distant rocky outcrop above the village. They would give his team cover when they entered the village, and watch out for Taliban movements, especially on the main road. He removed his sunglasses, before grabbing his M4 carbine from Master Sergeant Ben Saunders. Connor issued instructions, "Jacko and Sam, you stay with the vehicle. Be ready to evac at a moment's notice. Ben, Danny and Sparks, come with me. You all know what to do."

Connor led the way on foot. The sprawl of sand-coloured mud-brick buildings looked deserted, but he knew appearances could be deceptive. They walked slowly and purposefully. They kept their eyes peeled and their M4 carbines ready. Gradually, Connor's men spread out and took up defensive positions: Lieutenant Danny Crow lying on a flat roof, Ben crouching in a ditch, Sergeant Major Sparks in a doorway. Connor walked alone into a narrow, shadow-filled alley. At the end he entered a sunny, walled courtyard. A boy was kicking a ball about. Their eyes met. The boy let out a cry of fright and ran off.

A tall figure appeared in a doorway; a man in his mid-thirties, about Connor's age. His face was familiar. Connor called out. "Assif, is that you?"

"Yes, it is I." A surprised and delighted Assif Aziz beamed a welcoming smile. "Praise be to Allah. After all these years. Nathan, is it really you? Come in. Come in. Welcome to my humble home, dear friend."

As Connor lowered his M4, childhood memories flooded back. As boys he and Assif had become best buddies after Connor's dad saved Assif's mother's life when she'd fallen seriously ill.

"How is your father, Nathan?" Assif asked as they embraced.

"Fine. He often speaks fondly of his time over here working for the UN."

"They were good days, Nathan."

Connor nodded. As a boy he had spent two years alongside his father in Afghanistan. "Was that your son I saw outside?"

"Yes. His name is Hassan. He's a good boy. Tomorrow, I'm sending him south to stay with his Uncle Emil, near Kandahar. There is a fine school nearby. I want a better life for Hassan. Better than this." He gestured to his bleak surroundings. "You remember Emil?"

As they settled down onto large cushions, Connor nodded. "Yes, of course. Is it wise to send Hassan to stay with him?" He pulled a face. "Emil was always causing trouble. Hope he's changed — for Hassan's sake."

Assif laughed. "Emil is my brother. What can I say?" An awkward pause followed and his smile disappeared. "You should not have come here, Nathan. The Taliban may be watching."

"I know. Actually, that's why I am here," Connor replied. "Things are about to hot up between here and the border. We know your village is on the Taliban trail north. We need you to feed us intel on their comings and goings." He sensed the heavy weight his words suddenly

13

placed on Assif's shoulders. "I know it's a lot to ask, but we'll make it worth your while. A thousand bucks a month, and we'll pay for anything else you need; a new well, your own schoolhouse or repairs to the mosque. I guess you know what'll happen if you refuse. Your village may be targeted by ISAF, maybe even by air strikes. Even as we speak, a reconnaissance team has set up camp near here."

Assif cursed. "What use is money or a new schoolhouse to dead men?" His tone dripped bitterness. "It's the same story in every village, Nathan. Soldiers come and tell us to grow wheat instead of opium. And that we must inform them should any Taliban pass through. But by sunset the soldiers are gone. Left alone, we are defenceless. Then in the night the Taliban come and make demands too. Like you, they threaten us. They punish us if we don't grow poppies for their opium. They punish us if we talk to you. It's the complete opposite and we cannot win." He threw up his arms in surrender.

Connor understood the awful dilemma he'd brought to the village and to his old friend's home. All over Afghanistan thousands of farmers like Assif were chained to poverty and stuck in the middle of a land that had only known war for hundreds of years. They were always in the wrong place at the wrong time, but had nowhere else to go. Connor knew he had some persuading to do.

*   *   *   *   *   *

Outside in the fields, Hassan saw the American soldiers watching him from the rocky outcrop. Nervously, the barefoot boy pushed his heavy wooden handcart along the rutted path between the poppy fields, picking up fist-sized stones as he went. He wanted to leave the cart and run, but there was nowhere to hide. Hassan didn't want to catch their attention — they might scramble down to talk to him. Maybe they'd yell and point their rifles. Or chew him out for being uncooperative. Would they shoot him? "*Inshallah*," he muttered aloud — if Allah wills it. He tried to imagine what it would feel like to get shot, and wondered whether it was better if a bullet passed right through him rather than it getting lodged inside his belly. On the other hand, they might give him a bar of chocolate. The infidels always had lots of tempting bars of delicious chocolate. Hassan knelt down, picked up another stone, and dropped it into his cart. The distant roar of engines made Hassan turn and shield his eyes. He spotted a rising trail of dust amid the shimmering heat. Three red Toyota pickups sped past on the main road, heading south. He watched them until they were out of view. Taliban, he suspected. He was curious as to why the Americans hadn't opened fire.

Hassan began wheeling his cart full of stones back to his village. Had the Americans come to blow up his house? he fretted. He also knew that the Taliban sometimes blew up houses; but mostly they slit throats or cut off heads. Anyone who didn't do as they were told, or who made friends with the American infidels, would suffer. They're all crazy, Hassan decided. All of them.

He heard a strange noise, and looked up into the sky. It was a drone. He'd never seen one so close, and this one was heading his way. It was flying as if it was out of control, like it was being flown by a drunken pilot. Then he saw the missile spark into life and accelerate away, leaving a trail across the sky. Hassan gulped. Was he the target? He dropped to his knees, crawled behind his cart and prayed. The missile flashed overhead and a moment later smacked into the outcrop.

A blinding flash. A deafening, earth-shaking

crump. The pressure wave toppled Hassan's cart, knocking him flat and scattering the stones. A mushroom cloud of black smoke rose hundreds of metres into the air. Rubble, dirt and debris rained down. A set of dog tags and a severed arm landed close to where Hassan lay.

Shaken, he stood up and dusted himself down. He stared at the arm; the fingers were still twitching. Somehow, it didn't look real. Slightly dazed, he picked up the dog tags. The name on them read: Brad Somersby. It doesn't make sense, Hassan thought. Why would the Americans bomb their own patrol? Without thinking, he put the dog tags into his pocket.

CHAPTER THREE
Connor's promise

The explosion from the Hellfire missile shook
Assif's house. Dust fell from the ceiling. Startled,
Assif leaped to his feet. Connor snatched his
radio from his trouser cargo pocket. "Sparks,
what the hell is going on out there, over?"

Silence.

"Sparks? Do you read me, over?"

Eventually, Connor's radio crackled into life.
Sparks's voice sounded odd. "S-s-sir, something
terrible has happened. One of our drones has
taken out Halo, over."

"What?" Connor sprang to his feet too.
"Repeat that, over."

"The whole hillside, sir, it's...it's gone! Over."
Connor gaped in a mix of astonishment and
horror. His brain could barely grasp what had
happened. Then Jacko radioed in from the Humvee.

"Sir, we've got company too. Insurgents heading
in from the east, over."

Connor had to think fast but calmly. Years
of combat experience kicked in. "Roger that.
Everyone evac now. Get your butts back to the
Humvee, over." He turned to Assif. "Gotta go, old
friend. Think about what I've said."

Reluctantly, Assif nodded. "First, I must speak to the village elders. I shall organise a shura, an informal meeting of the village council. They may have their own demands. And, Nathan, they will want to look you in the eye and see that your promises of help are truthful. Return tomorrow evening, then you shall have our decision."

Connor nodded.

"As for myself, I shall recommend that we assist you. For old time's sake." Assif smiled awkwardly. "But I have one demand of my own."

"Go on," said Connor, heading for the door.

"Should anything happen to me, promise that you will seek out Hassan and make sure he's OK. Do what you can for him."

Connor paused in the doorway and held out a hand. "You have my word."

*   *   *   *   *   *

The following evening Connor and his team headed back to Assif's village to hear their decision. As they drew closer they saw smoke rising into a rapidly darkening sky. "Don't stop," Connor ordered, the contents of his stomach suddenly feeling leaden. "Drive into the village."

The Humvee crawled slowly up the main street. Connor stared at the burned-out buildings. "Wait here," he ordered, leaping from the vehicle and heading up the alley.

Assif's body lay in the courtyard in a pool of sticky blood. His throat had been cut. The Taliban had come and wreaked revenge against the villagers for daring to talk to the Americans. Connor sank to his knees next to his dead friend. "This is my fault," he said, choked. "You were right, Assif, old friend, I shouldn't have come." Peering around, he called out desperately, "Hassan? Hassan?"

CHAPTER FOUR
Search for intel

Kandahar

News of the marines in Halo Forward Patrol killed in action travelled fast. Photos and names filled every newspaper and TV news channel across the world. Most reports were vague about just what exactly had happened. With facts thin on the ground, rumours of a friendly fire incident spread quickly.

Connor knew the truth would come out before long. It always did. But for now, no one was quite sure exactly what had happened. With the Predator drone missing, along with the remainder of its Hellfire missiles, Central Command was desperate for information. Connor reckoned he knew just the man to talk to. Dressing native to blend in with the locals of Kandahar, Connor wore a long white cotton shirt and white cotton trousers. The turban on his head was expertly wrapped — the result of years of practice in front of a mirror. With a deep tan, decent beard growth, and speaking fluent Pashto, few eyed him with more than the usual suspicion.

Connor pressed through Kandahar's crowded

bazaar, passing stalls selling everything from pirated DVDs, jerry cans of fuel, to slabs of slowly rotting meat swarming with flies. Connor's senses buzzed — the Taliban had surely infiltrated the bazaar. Chatter filled his ears; heated arguments, determined bartering for the best price. The air reeked with a mix of hot spices and excrement; every house ditched its human waste into the nearby stream, and in the same foul waters Connor saw women wash clothes and children splash and play.

Connor arrived at a market stall flogging old car radios, guarded by a dumb-looking youth with sharp eyes and an even sharper tongue.

"Is your grandfather here, Mushtaq?" Connor asked.

Mushtaq stared at Connor like he'd seen a ghost, then cursed him at length before finally nodding and gesturing to an open doorway covered by a striped cloth. Connor pushed past him and entered the dusty brick building. He blinked to adjust his eyes to the gloom and observed Mushtaq's grandfather, Abdul, sitting cross-legged on a mattress and dribbling chewed tobacco into a spittoon. Most of it ended up on his long grey beard. They exchanged greetings and Abdul beckoned Connor to sit.

"Mushtaq!" the old man yelled. "Bring us tea!" He turned his attention to Connor. "So, the rumours are all lies. You're still alive, Major Connor. Last I heard you'd got into a spot of bother at Lashkar-Gah. It was reported that one of the local warlords stuck your head on a pole outside his tent." Abdul chuckled. "Is this an official visit because I know nothing about those stolen rocket-propelled grenades?"

"Nice to see you too, you old rogue," Connor replied. "Relax. I'm just after some intel. We lost one of our birds."

Abdul grinned. "So I heard."

"Thought you might have. You know everything that goes on within a hundred mile radius of this dump. You and I are the same, Abdul, we're both fixers. It's our job to keep our fingers on the pulse."

Mushtaq breezed in carrying a tray. He set it down on a rug and, in silence, poured two cups of steaming tea. Abdul waited for him to leave before announcing, "I can be of no assistance, I'm afraid, Major Connor."

"But you know what happened to our drone."

"Of course."

Connor drew a wad of greenbacks from his pocket. "There's five K. Another five if it's where you say it is."

Abdul shrugged and remained silent.

Connor easily read the old man like a cheap comic. Abdul's silence meant only one thing. Death by a thousand cuts might come in the night to the person who gave up such a secret freely. Connor cranked up the pressure. "Sorry, Abdul, but this is serious. Here, keep the five." He tossed the cash into the old man's lap. "Now, tell me everything otherwise I'll have this dump bulldozed. And I know where you hide your stash of AK-47s, and I have no doubt half those car radios you sell get broken up and the bits used to wire up IEDs. I'll have you arrested and you'll spend the next twenty years behind bars. That village idiot grandson of yours, Mushtaq, too."

Abdul's watery black eyes met Connor's unblinking stare. "You have changed, Major Connor. A year ago you would have left here empty-handed. I see that will not happen this time. You are growing more like me with every sunrise." He began to shake with laughter.

Connor sipped his sugared tea as the old man revealed what he knew in whispers so quiet they had Connor leaning forward and straining to hear.

"Masud, the local Taliban leader here, and his men have gained access to technology matching yours, Major Connor. It is said they can block your satellite transmissions and hack all of your encryption codes. They took over control of your Predator and used it against your own men. They are your equals. You must be very afraid."

"Masud! Should've guessed." Connor slumped back. Masud was top of their Most Wanted list. In truth, he felt startled at hearing his worst fears confirmed but he hid his concern well. His superiors had clung on to the vain hope that Predator Alpha One had simply malfunctioned, loosed a wayward missile that had the misfortune to kill the marines in Halo Forward Patrol, and then flown until it ran out of fuel and crashed. No such luck. The reality was terrifying. The Taliban had an operational drone armed with Hellfire missiles. And it was going to be Delta Force's job to sort it.

Abdul sighed. "Special Forces will soon have more blood on their hands, I fear, *inshallah*... Head for the hills, Major Connor. To the north. To where the sun never shines. Look for the scorpion's tail. There you will find what you seek."

"Can't you be more precise?" Connor snapped. Abdul always spoke in riddles.

Abdul shrugged. "That is all I know. You have a brain, Major Connor. Figure it out."

The chirping ring of Abdul's mobile phone interrupted the meeting. Abdul picked it up and listened without saying a word. Eventually he placed the phone back down and called out, "Mushtaq, pack everything away. We're closing early today."

Connor had been deep in thought. "They must have some sort of landing strip and somewhere to hide both the drone and their equipment. They'd need a pretty powerful transmitter too. And where the sun never shines probably means a very deep valley always in shadow." The bit about the scorpion's tail had him stumped — for now.

Abdul rose to his feet. "I congratulate you, Major Connor. Now, I think it best if you leave here quickly. Avoid the bazaar. Best if you take the backstreets. Mushtaq can show you the way if you like."

Connor got up too but hesitated. "There's something else. A different matter. I'm looking for someone. A boy called Hassan. He's twelve. I think he might be living with his uncle somewhere around here, a man called Emil Aziz. I made a promise to an old friend."

Abdul grew impatient. "Yes, yes, very well." Abdul took Connor's arm and ushered him towards the doorway. "You really must leave now."

"OK, but the boy, Hassan. Will you make enquiries? I'll throw in an extra couple of grand."

"I'll ask around, Major Connor. Give me your cell phone number and I'll text you if I find out anything."

Outside Connor shielded his eyes from the bright sunlight. From the top of the local mosque's tall minaret the voice of a muezzin called the faithful to afternoon prayer. Connor quickly realised Mushtaq had already cleared the stall and was nowhere to be seen. At the far end of the street he spotted an ISAF patrol, ten soldiers in desert combat fatigues, MICHs (Modular Integrated Communications Helmets), SPEAR (Special Operations Forces Equipment Advanced Requirements) protective vests, and armed with standard issue M4 carbines. One was crouching at the corner offering covering fire. The others walked slowly forward in distinctly relaxed mode – a friendly presence aimed at winning hearts and minds. Gangs of unruly kids swarmed about them demanding gifts with outstretched hands that quickly filled with bars of chocolate.

Connor had this weird feeling – something wasn't right. The phone call. The hurried closing of the stall. Abdul's sense of urgency. The appearance of an ISAF patrol. Connor added them all up and was filled with alarm. His heart began racing as he frantically searched the crowd with his eyes. Innocent people were about to die. He had to do something – fast.

CHAPTER FIVE
Bomber in the bazaar

Connor moved into the crowd, looking for a particular face — someone nervous, or sweating, or with a glazed stare. His focus locked on to a young man walking slowly and deliberately towards the ISAF patrol. It was his eyes that gave him away; they were the eyes of a suicide bomber. The target was keeping to the gap between the market stalls and the buildings. Connor had to act with precision. The slightest error and he'd be blown up along with everyone else. He overtook the bomber and dipped into the dark shadow of a doorway. Ideally, he'd prefer to take the bomber alive. But the man could have several kilos of plastic explosive strapped to his belly. Connor couldn't risk giving him the chance to detonate it. The man passed the door and Connor struck, reaching out, one arm wrapping around his neck, his other hand gripping his chin — a quick, forceful twist, a snap of vertebrae, and job done. Connor let the body slump against him and he pulled it inside. Under the man's shirt was a vest packed with explosives. He pulled the detonator out. "No martyrdom for you, son, not today, not ever."

CHAPTER SIX
Search for the Predator

Camp Delta

Returning to Camp Delta, situated thirty miles
from Kandahar, Connor arrived at the same
moment a Chinook touched down, its twin sets
of rotors kicking up a sandstorm. Head of Central
Command, General Patterson, emerged from
the helo flanked by senior intelligence staff and
several CIA operatives.

Busy fixing a new swivel mounting for a large calibre machine gun to one of their vehicles, Ben looked up and whistled. "Hey, there you are Major Connor, sir. Sergeant Sparks is looking for you. Our orders are to assemble in the Ops Room as soon as they arrive. Looks like you got back just in time." Wiping the grease from his hands with an oil rag, he jumped down and gazed at the general and his men and whistled. "Judging by the number of stars on show something distinctly brown, wet and smelly has hit the fan."

"I think you're right, Ben. Round up the others."

General Patterson paced the cramped Ops Room, repeatedly mopping the sweat from the back of his neck with a handkerchief while listening. Connor's men sat in silence too, as their commander relayed the intel gleaned from Abdul at the bazaar. "What you've learned fits in with our latest intercepts, Major," said one of the CIA operatives. "There's a lot of excited cell phone chatter going on out there."

"Sir, there's something I don't understand," said Sam Wilson. At just nineteen, Sam was the youngest of Connor's team, but had already seen action in Iraq. His sniper skills were the best Connor had seen. "If the drone was taken, surely we'd have tracked it on radar."

General Patterson shook his head. "Nope, son, hills got in the way. Anyway, it was a new stealth version of the Predator."

"Oh, great." Danny folded his arms and looked up at the canvas ceiling. "An invisible needle in the world's largest haystack."

Another of the CIA men interrupted. "The drone was equipped with a precision global satellite positioning device, of course, but whoever took control of it switched it off."

Connor's team started murmuring to one another, assuming someone, somewhere, had messed up big time. General Patterson called them to order. "Major Connor, in a week from now our president is going to make a surprise visit to troops based at Kandahar to provide a much needed boost to morale. With luck, it'll give the papers something to write about other than body bags being flown home. Naturally, a rogue Predator armed with Hellfire missiles represents a major security threat. That threat must be neutralised. You have one week, Major. Our butts are on the line. Just tell me what you need and you'll get it."

Connor looked at his men. They were a highly skilled team. He'd hand-picked every one of them. With the help of one or two helicopter gunships they could take out the Predator and the Taliban base. All he needed was its location. "Sir, I want satellite imagery of all possible landing sites in the mountains. Old pictures too, if you have them, so we can make comparisons. Plus any phone intercepts or other intel that might narrow the search area. Once we've found the base, fly us in and we'll get the job done."

Patterson grimaced. "Doesn't sound like much of a plan."

"Well, it's the best on offer."

*   *   *   *   *   *

Shielding their eyes, Connor and his men watched the Chinook climb slowly into the air and turn away, carrying General Patterson and his entourage back to Base Command near Kabul. "Sir, what is it? You look worried," asked Sparks.

"I don't believe in coincidences," Connor replied. "A drone being taken just before a surprise visit by our president? The Taliban know he's coming. I'm sure of it. But what worries me most is that they won't cancel his visit — they never do — whatever the threat. There's too much at stake. And that means we mustn't fail."

CHAPTER SEVEN
Hassan escapes

A village outside Kandahar

The Taliban crept silently from the hills and entered the village just after midnight. They knocked on Hassan's uncle's door and entered. Woken by the noise, Hassan hid under his blanket and listened.

Hassan had only been at his uncle's house for two days, when news of his father's murder reached him. He had not spoken since, and refused to go to his new school. Instead, he wandered around his uncle's farm, where he could cry on his own. On one occasion Hassan's uncle had caught him crying in the house and beaten him for what Emil said was "weakness". Emil told him coldly that what had happened to his father was merely punishment for working with the Americans. Hassan didn't understand. His father hadn't asked the Amercians to come. What if the Taliban in the next room were the same ones who'd slit his father's throat? Had they come to do the same to him?

Eventually, curiosity got the better of him. He tiptoed to within earshot. Then, carefully

peeking through a hole in a curtain separating
the rooms, he saw the infamous Taliban leader,
Masud. In the lamplight Hassan could see his richly
tanned face beneath a black turban, and skin so
wrinkled it looked painful. His dark eyes frightened
Hassan. He listened as his uncle pleaded.

"But that's not enough money to see me through the winter, Masud. All of my opium harvest and half my food stores for so little. Please, sir, a man must live. And I have an extra mouth to feed."

"An extra mouth? Explain," Masud snapped.

"My brother's son, sir. He's travelled here from the north to go to the school in Kandahar. His father was friendly with the American infidels and the Taliban there killed him, and everyone else in the village for his treachery. I am the only family the poor boy has now."

Masud spat a lump of half-chewed naan bread from his mouth and cursed. "The boy must die, too. Otherwise one day he will avenge his father's death. Where is he?"

Filled with renewed fright, Hassan cowered.

"Allah have mercy. Please, sir, let the boy live... Anyway, I'll need his help to harvest my poppy fields if I'm to have your opium ready in time for your return. Alone, it cannot be done. I'll keep him off school to work the fields."

Masud stared thoughtfully at Emil. "Very well. Keep the boy here. He can help you deliver your harvest. We shall let him live until we return. Then he must die."

Hassan crept quickly to his room and gathered

up his few possessions in a blanket. One thought occupied his head — to run away in case they changed their minds and decided to kill him now. He climbed out of his window and dropped softly onto the earth outside. Looking round he saw other Taliban on watch; one on the roof of a building opposite, one on the wall, another lurking in the alleyway. Keeping low, he ducked into the poppy fields, using the tall flower stems for cover. There he lay on his belly, trembling. And as he waited for the Taliban to go, a crushing reality dawned on him. He had nowhere to run. There was nobody he could trust. He was alone.

As he watched the Taliban leave, his fear faded and was replaced by a growing anger. Men like them had ruined his life and murdered those he loved. He knew nothing would ever change while they roamed about spreading terror. Slowly his anger changed to thoughts of revenge. If he knew where the Taliban camp was, he could tell the Americans. They would come and get rid of them. That would be just revenge. Hassan knelt on his kness and offered up prayers; that Allah would protect him, that Allah would show him the way, that Allah would let him succeed. Carefully he got to his feet and began walking, following in the footsteps of the Taliban.

CHAPTER EIGHT
Painful memories

Camp Delta

As well as Connor and his team, Camp Delta was temporary home to several hundred soldiers of the renowned 101st US Airborne Division. It was a sun-baked sprawl of tents, cargo containers and temporary structures housing pizza and hamburger outlets, all surrounded by Hesco fortifications; wire structures filled with rocks, sand and concrete. Security was tight. Incoming mortar fire was an almost daily occurrence.

Connor paused by the makeshift memorial to the fallen in the central parade ground and studied the list of names. The most recent additions were those of Halo Forward Patrol, including Brad Somersby... Connor was in a reflective mood.

"You wanted to see me, Major Connor."

Startled, Connor spun round. "Yes, padre."

"What can I do for you?"

Every camp had a padre — or army chaplain — who ran church services. They were often the ones soldiers turned to when they wanted to talk about personal problems — in confidence. Connor glanced both ways to make sure no one was in earshot. He felt awkward — he hated the idea of appearing weak. "I've been having a recurring nightmare, sir. They started about a month ago. Haven't had nightmares since I was a kid. And they're getting worse."

"I see. Tell you what, let's go grab a cup of coffee in my quarters."

In the privacy of the padre's hot stuffy tent, Connor spoke of how every night he dreamed of raiding a village. Then he would frantically search house after house, but everyone was lying dead in pools of blood. He always awoke drenched in sweat. The padre listened carefully, but then coaxed out of Connor the trigger for his night terrors: the death of his friend, Assif.

"You blame yourself for his death," the padre declared with conviction. "Such guilt is a normal reaction. It wasn't your fault and you know it, but sometimes that's not enough."

"But will the nightmares go away?"

"Time is a great healer, Major. They will fade. I'm sure of it. And you mustn't see it as a weakness. You may be a highly trained soldier and taught to act instinctively, to kill the enemy without a second's thought, but never forget the most important thing."

"And what's that?"

"You're still human, Major."

"But what can I do to stop them?"

The padre shrugged. "Hard to say. Finding that boy Hassan might do it."

"Thank you. You've been a great help, sir." Connor got up from his canvas chair and shook the padre's hand.

The padre grasped Connor's hand tightly and stared into his face. "You had a son, didn't you, Major? If my memory is correct he was killed in a hit and run back home. Must be two years ago now?" He waited to see how Connor would react.

Nodding slowly, Connor broke free from the padre's grip. "Yes. Almost three years ago. I was in Iraq at the time."

"I see. Must've been very difficult for you, especially so far away from home. Listen, if you need to talk, Major, I'm always here, 24-7."

"Thanks, but that won't be necessary, sir."

Connor strode back towards the Ops Room filled with a renewed determination to find Hassan.

The padre flipped open his notebook and wrote: "Major Connor — early signs of instability. Possibly battle fatigue but more likely personal matters, maybe elements of post-traumatic stress. Keep a close eye on him."

CHAPTER NINE
Captured

Foothills of Afghan mountains

For three days and nights Hassan followed the Taliban as they moved from village to village. There they collected food and negotiated deals for their drugs, to sell over the border or exchange for guns. At one stop they took two donkeys and used them to carry supplies. Hassan stole what little food he had to in order to survive.

They travelled on, keeping to hidden trails and deep gullies, and frequently they posted spotters. Hassan had to tread carefully, never getting too close or dropping back too far in case he lost sight of them.

Slowly the journey took him into the foothills. Tall mountains seemed to grow higher with every step. As he followed Masud and his men, Hassan drew his own map, marking villages and landmarks. He'd need it to find his way back. Hot days turned into freezing nights, and Hassan slept under the stars wrapped in his blanket. On the fourth morning he woke up aching all over. He shivered and cursed the Taliban with their warm campfires and steaming cups of tea. Around him lay barren rock and loose scree shrouded in the early morning mist. Suddenly he felt something prod his back. He rolled over. A young Taliban fighter stood over him holding an AK-47 rifle.

Hassan was dragged kicking and screaming to the Taliban's overnight camp. He was taken straight to their leader — Masud.

"Why have you been following us?"

Hassan had to think fast. Masud clutched a knife and had evil in his eyes. "I want to join you," Hassan lied, unconvincingly. The blade was quickly at his throat. Hassan flinched. "That's the truth. I want to fight the American infidel. To kill them all." This time he sounded more believable.

"What is your name?"

"Hassan, sir."

The threatening expression on Masud's face softened and then he grinned toothlessly. "Hassan, Hassan," he repeated over and over. "You are a gift from Allah. You will have your chance to martyr yourself for our cause. We shall take you under our wing and teach you all we know. And for you, young Hassan, Paradise will come soon. Very soon." He seized Hassan by the shoulder. "But first you can look after our stubborn donkeys for us. They don't seem to share your enthusiasm."

CHAPTER TEN
Scorpion Valley

Camp Delta

Blood. So much blood. Blood everywhere.

Connor woke in a sweat. Sparks was leaning over him. "Nate, are you all right?"

Blinking away the nightmare, Connor sat up on the edge of his camp bed. It was eight o'clock in the morning, and he could already feel the heat outside. "Yeah, I'm fine. What's going on?"

"We think we've made a breakthrough."

Connor and Sparks hurried over to Camp Delta's Ops Room. The tables were littered with laptops, satellite photos, air reconnaissance pictures, maps, empty Coke cans and half-eaten pizzas. "We've been working all night, sir," said a tired but beaming Danny Crow. "We've spoken to Army Intelligence, the CIA, and Central Command's Comms section. We narrowed down the landing sites and reckon we've found it."

Connor studied the maps and photographs that had been set out for him.

Crow pointed to the middle picture. "See that? The valley's shaped like a scorpion's tail. It opens up onto a plain where there's a dried-up river bed. Now look at this picture taken two months ago. It's different. Someone's straightened out part of the river bed — like a landing strip. It's located about forty miles from here."

Connor could see it now and smiled. He remembered Abdul's riddle about the scorpion's tail in the north. "So where's our bird?"

"Here, sir." Danny tapped a finger. "There's a massive rock overhang at the entrance to the valley. We think it's hidden underneath, where

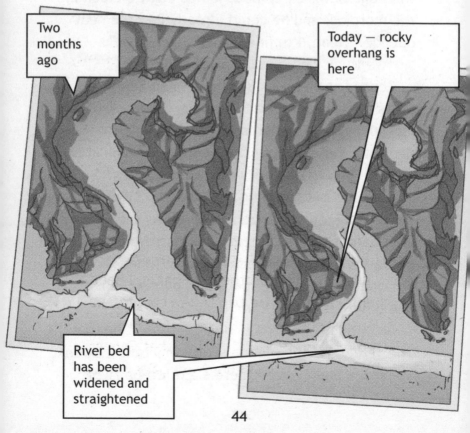

Two months ago

Today — rocky overhang is here

River bed has been widened and straightened

there are also caves perfect for hiding all their gear. Guys over at Comms said they're probably transmitting and controlling the drone from a mobile unit — like a truck."

Ben added, "They chose the valley well. It is so narrow that an air strike is unlikely to work, even using deep penetration JDAM bombs, sir."

Connor felt his cell phone vibrate. He took it out and checked the text message. Abdul had a possible address for Hassan's uncle. Instantly, Connor's mind drifted to thinking about Hassan.

"Sir?"

Connor saw his men looking at him expectantly. "Good work, team. This is our target. Now, let's find our best insertion point — we go in tomorrow night and hit them hard at dawn. Jacko, you're in charge of putting a plan together. Ben, inform General Patterson of our progress, and tell him that I'll speak to him this evening, when I'm back."

"Back from where?" asked Ben.

"I've got something to sort out." Connor turned to Sparks. They'd fought together for over ten years, and were like brothers. "Sparks, I need your help. Fancy a little trip to the country, no questions asked?"

Sparks smiled. He didn't know what Connor had planned, but he would always back him up.

CHAPTER ELEVEN
Masud's plan

Masud's hidden base — Scorpion Valley

At first, Hassan prodded the stubborn donkeys with a stick, but gradually they became easier to lead. They were walking over a flattened river bed when suddenly Masud stopped, turned and announced, "We are here, Hassan. This is where you will live from now on. Come."

Masud led Hassan into the shadows beneath a huge overhanging rock. There, Hassan gazed awestruck at the smooth grey paint of a Predator drone. Men moved busily to and fro carrying equipment to a parked truck that somehow they'd managed to drive across the rough terrain of the plain. Hassan couldn't recall seeing anything resembling a road for miles.

Masud caressed the nose casing of a Hellfire missile. "You will share in our joy, Hassan. Soon, very soon, we shall strike at the heart of the American infidel. Their president, Hassan. He is coming here, and here he shall die. Just imagine. Men will see our victory and rise up. They will know that Allah is with us. We shall drive out the infidels. Our country will be free once more.

And you, Hassan, will play your part. Now go and fetch me some tea."

Hassan suddenly understood what had happened back home in his village. The Americans hadn't attacked their own. It was the Taliban's doing. They had blown up the soldiers on the rocky outcrop. It was Masud's drone now. Moving beyond the overhang he saw numerous openings to caves. Inside, fires had been lit and men were cooking food, cleaning their rifles and planning operations. There were weapons everywhere: rifles, rocket-propelled grenades, boxes of ammunition. He counted maybe forty men in total, and heard various languages being spoken. Many had travelled far to fight for their cause. As he watched tea being poured, he began to plan his escape.

It would have to be at night. His map would show him the way. It had to. If he got lost he might starve or die of thirst. But would he get back in time to warn the Americans? It was a long way and he was already exhausted. I know, he thought, I shall take food, water and a donkey. I shall lead him from here quietly in the dead of night and ride him down through the foothills.

Hassan knew that if they caught him creeping away, Masud would kill him.

CHAPTER TWELVE
Tracing Hassan

Emil's home, just outside Kandahar

Connor grabbed Hassan's uncle by the throat. "What do you mean Hassan's disappeared?"

"Sir, go easy on him," said Sparks, surprised at his commander's loss of control.

Connor released his grip. "I'm not leaving until I've got some answers. Now, Emil, start talking, or you can kiss your opium crop goodbye." He saw the look of horror on Emil's face. "I'll burn every last damn poppy — and I bet the Taliban offered you a good price? Yes, of course they did."

"Please, there have been no Taliban here, sir. Not for six months. I hate the Taliban as much as you do."

"So where's Hassan?"

"What do you want with the boy? And how is it you know my name?"

Connor resisted the urge to strike the man with his fist. "I know you, Emil. And I never did like you. Not when we were kids. Not now. You and your brother Assif are like chalk and cheese. In my book the wrong man's dead. Don't you recognise me?"

48

Astonished and confused, Emil peered into Connor's eyes. "Nathan? Nathan Connor?"

Connor ground his teeth and nodded. Even as boys they'd fought. He'd even once caught Emil stealing money from his father's wallet. He didn't trust the man standing before him further than he could throw him.

Emil threw up his arms. "All right, all right. Allah protect me, I'll tell you, Nathan. Yes, the Taliban did come here. On the same night Hassan disappeared."

"They took him?"

"No, Nathan. I think he ran away. I let slip that his father had been killed for collaborating with you Americans. The Taliban leader wanted the boy dead but I persuaded him to let him live. I said I needed his help here on the farm."

"Then why did he run away?" Sparks asked, as confused as Connor was.

Emil diverted his eyes in shame. "They said they'd kill him on their return. The boy must've overheard."

"Oh great!" Connor clenched his fist. "So he could be anywhere. Absolutely anywhere."

CHAPTER THIRTEEN
Delta Force move in

Masud's hidden base — Scorpion Valley

As night fell Hassan was put to work serving food to the Taliban huddled around their campfires. He did what they asked. But he also listened to their plans; how the truck would be driven to within a few miles of Kandahar, and from there the drone would be controlled. He realised that they knew exactly when the American president would arrive and where he'd be during his visit.

It was after midnight before he managed to slip outside the cave. But before he could escape he heard footsteps. "Hassan?" It was Masud.

"Tell me about your family, Hassan, about your father. Is he one of us, too?" Masud had a tight hold of Hassan's arm.

"He's dead. He was a good man and I miss him."

"Then you shall call me father. Come, it is late. Tomorrow I shall begin teaching you. But now you must sleep."

Hassan had no choice. His escape would have to wait one more day.

*　　　*　　　*　　　*　　　*　　　*

The Black Hawk helicopter flew low and fast through the darkness. Using night-vision goggles the pilot climbed up the valley and hovered within metres of a narrow ledge. Connor and his team jumped out.

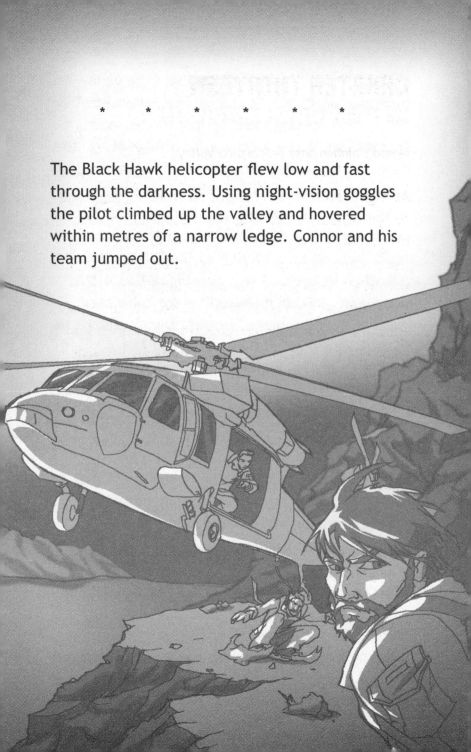

Delta Force's insertion point was the valley next to their target. It reduced the chances of the Taliban hearing their helicopter approach. Quickly they made their way to a ridge above the base. Using infrared and thermal-imaging scopes attached to their helmets they scanned the scorpion-shaped valley beyond for signs of life. Up to this moment, Connor didn't know if his team had correctly identified the Taliban base. But when he spotted two glowing specks — the body heat of Taliban lookouts — he knew they were in the right place. He sent Danny and Jacko to deal with them — silently.

"OK, Sam, you know what to do. Position yourself with a maximum field of fire," said Connor.

Sam headed off, clutching his M110A1 semi-automatic 7.62mm sniper rifle.

Connor and the remainder of his team — Sparks and Ben — moved down the side of the valley. Each of them wore lightweight multi-hit body armour, and carried a modified M4 carbine. Connor's had a visible laser marker, vertical forward grip, and quick detachable silencer. Sparks had gone for a tactical sight and silencer, while Ben opted for a shortened barrel and grenade launcher. It was five o'clock in the morning when they reached a gully close to the mouth of the valley. An hour later, Danny and Jacko rejoined them. Using their infrared scopes they could see beneath the rock overhang and make out the shapes of the Predator drone and truck. "Off you go, Sparks," Connor whispered. "Ben, you go with him. We'll cover you. Lay those explosive charges and set the timers for first light at precisely six forty-five."

As Sparks and Ben crept off, Connor spoke into his tactical radio. "Command, this is Delta Force. Have located target bird. Party time is zero-six-four-five. Please confirm air support, over."

His radio crackled. "Roger that, Delta Force. Two DAP (Direct Action Penetrator) helicopter gunships will mop up and your evac will be by Black Hawk helicopter at previously agreed co-ordinates, over."

Out of breath, Sparks returned twenty minutes later, Ben right on his heels. They rolled down into the gulley. "All set, sir."

CHAPTER FOURTEEN
Party time

Hassan was determined to make his escape.
But there was a problem. One of Masud's men
blocked the cave's exit. Hassan despaired but the
urge to flee was strong. He didn't want to spend
another day shooting at tin cans and learning how
to blow people up.

It wasn't until nearly six o'clock in the morning
that finally the young Taliban fighter appeared to
fall asleep. Hassan got up and tiptoed outside,
carrying his blanket. At least it was still dark,
he thought. And quiet too. He made his way to
where the donkeys were tethered. He slung his
few possessions onto the back of the beast that
had given him the least trouble on his journey
to the camp. He led it away, stopping to prod its
backside with a stick every time its stubbornness
returned. Hassan prayed to Allah to keep him
safe as he followed a winding path that led to
a deep gulley. If he could just reach the gulley,
with any luck he'd be able to leave the valley
unseen, even after dawn. As he walked, he
couldn't help but feel all shaky, hollow-bellied,
and sick. One wrong move, the slightest sound,
and he'd be dead.

* * * * * *

Pressed huddled against the dirt wall of the gulley, Connor and his team readied themselves, clicking off their safety catches and flipping up their night-vision aids. Sparks studied the second hand of his watch. The first glimmers of dawn lit the sky. He counted down the seconds... Ten... Nine... Eight... "Sir, it's time to party."

Beneath the rock overhang the explosives detonated, blasting fragments of the drone more than two hundred metres, accompanied by twisted parts of the Taliban's truck. Connor issued the order to attack.

Rising up, he strained to see through the billowing clouds of dust, but as the air cleared the entrances to the nearby caves came into view. Taliban fighters streamed out of them like termites from a nest. Connor took aim and fired in short bursts. Danny Crow began shooting grenades from his modified rifle. From his elevated position higher up the side of the valley, Sam picked off the enemy, his double taps — two quick shots in a row — were deadly accurate.

Within thirty seconds the mayhem was joined by the rhythmical thwacking of helicopter rotor blades as two MH-60L DAP gunships flew in low and fast from the plain. Rockets streamed from their wing pods, and tracer fire flashed from their side-mounted miniguns. The valley was set alight with blinding and deafening explosions.

"Mission accomplished," Connor shouted. "Start our withdrawal." Into his radio he bellowed, "Sam, get your butt down to the evac co-ordinates, over."

"Roger that, Major. I have a visual on our helo. ETA touchdown in one minute, over."

*   *   *   *   *   *

A blast threw Hassan onto his belly. Dazed, he struggled to his feet while bullets fizzed past him. His donkey had bolted and Hassan knew he would have to catch the beast — he'd never escape without it. So he ran into the darkness, pumping his arms and forcing his legs to go faster.

Dust and smoke blew into the gulley like a sandstorm, and Hassan was quickly disorientated. But still he ran — and almost died of fright when he clattered into a figure crouching low. Hassan simply didn't see him.

"Hassan, there you are."

Blood oozed from a wound on Masud's shoulder, but the Taliban leader still managed to grab Hassan's arm tightly. He grinned toothlessly. "Come, boy, I know another way out of here."

"No!" Hassan shrieked as he tried to break free.

"Don't be afraid, little Hassan. You and I shall live to fight another day. Come with me, now, and don't cry out. Come, come, there's very little time."

CHAPTER FIFTEEN
Time to go

"Helo's touching down, sir," Ben shouted. "Time to evac."

Connor had covered his men's withdrawal, but was now staring into the grey-brown dust clouds filling the gulley. He could hear something odd. And it was coming towards him — fast. Snatching his rifle to his shoulder he took aim. "Get going, Ben, I'll be right behind you."

Connor's finger caressed the trigger and then began to squeeze it as the shape emerged from the swirling blur and he recalled one of the best pieces of advice he'd ever been given — never, ever, trust an Afghan donkey.

The Taliban had many tricks, most learned during the mujahedin's victory against the Russians back in the 1980s. A donkey laden with explosives was a favourite. Send it among the enemy and detonate it by remote control. Connor didn't need to think twice. He drilled the beast with bullets.

As the donkey fell and rolled onto its back, the string broke and a goatskin filled with water burst. The rolled-up blanket unfurled and its contents spilled out. Connor saw a glint of something and was puzzled. Surely it couldn't be what he thought it was.

Cautiously, he approached the dead donkey. He grabbed up a pair of bloodstained US Army dog tags, and examined them. He could just make out a name — Brad Somersby. Connor remembered seeing that name on the memorial back at Camp Delta. Brad had been part of Halo Forward Patrol. But what were his dog tags doing here? Connor knelt down to pick something else up: a piece of folded paper from a school book that had been inside the blanket. He opened it up and stared at it. A hand-drawn map showed the route all the way from Emil's farm. On the other side was some school work from a pupil named Hassan Aziz. Connor stood up abruptly and gazed around. "Hassan...? Hassan! Where are you?"

Ben appeared at his shoulder. "Sir, we've gotta go. Our helo won't wait any longer."

"Goddamn it... Hassan!" Connor yelled. He made a snap decision and headed off.

Ben caught him up. "Sir, where the hell are you going? ... We must leave. Now!"

Reluctantly, Connor stopped then turned back. But as he headed for the waiting helicopter, one thought occupied his mind — *Hassan, I will find you.*

WEAPONS and GEAR

M4 CARBINE (5.56MM)
with Delta Force accessories

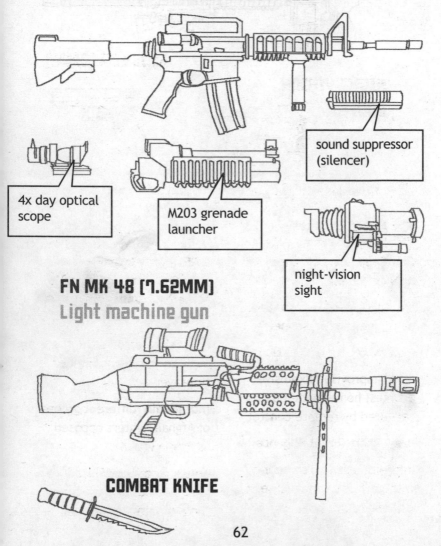

sound suppressor (silencer)

4x day optical scope

M203 grenade launcher

night-vision sight

FN MK 48 (7.62MM)
Light machine gun

COMBAT KNIFE

M110A1 (7.62MM)
Semi-automatic sniper system

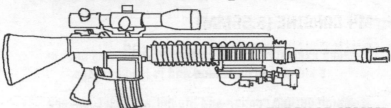

GLOCK 17 (9MM)

NIGHT-VISION SCOPE

GLOSSARY

CIA Central Intelligence Agency

dog tags identity tags worn by US military personnel

evac short for evacuation

IEDs Improvised Explosive Devices, home-made bombs triggered by remote control

intel short for intelligence

infidels refers to someone without faith, in this case, a non-Muslim

ISAF International Security Assistance Force – the NATO-led mission in Afghanistan

muezzin person at a mosque who leads the call to prayer

mujahedin different groups of Afghan fighters opposed to Russian rule

opium product created from poppies and used in the production of heroin

NEXT mission!

TASK FORCE DELTA
HOSTAGE CRISIS

More explosive action in Book 2, when a US doctor is kidnapped by Masud and is held hostage.

Major Nathan Connor and his Delta Force team are assigned to bring her back – alive.

Connor's instinct kicked in. The boy was telling him that there was another bomb inside the house. They were in the middle of a Taliban trap!

"Prepare for incoming," he warned his team. Had the convoy reached the site office and the bombs been detonated, there'd be no evac route — no way out.

Gunshots cracked from the hillside above. Danny let out a cry and sank to his knees. Connor grabbed Danny's webbing and began to drag him back towards the GMV. Jacko covered their backs, laying down a blanket of covering fire.

"Danny is hit," Connor announced into his helmet mic. "Ben, there's a second bomb in that house I've just passed. Hit it with everything you've got. Sparks, there are snipers up on the hillside. Call in our Hawks to take them out."

"Roger that, sir."

Continued in: Task Force Delta – Hostage Crisis